SUPER DC HEROES

BATMAN

ROBIN'S FIRST FLIGHT

WRITTEN BY
ROBERT GREENBERGER

ILLUSTRATED BY
GREGG SCHIGIEL AND
LEE LOUGHRIDGE

BATMAN CREATED BY
BOB KANE

Raintree

www.raintreepublishers.co.uk
Visit our website to find out
more information about
Raintree books.

To order:
☎ Phone 0845 6044371
🖷 Fax +44 (0) 1865 312263
🖳 Email myorders@raintreepublishers.co.uk

Customers from outside the UK please telephone +44 1865 312262

Raintree is an imprint of Capstone Global Library Limited,
a company incorporated in England and Wales having its registered office
at 7 Pilgrim Street, London, EC4V 6LB – Registered company number: 6695582

First published by Stone Arch Books in 2010
First published in the United Kingdom in hardback and paperback in 2010
The moral rights of the proprietor have been asserted.

Art Director: Bob Lentz
Designer: Brann Garvey
Production Specialist: Michelle Biedschied
Editor: Vaarunika Dharmapala
Originated by Capstone Global Library Ltd
Printed and bound in China by Leo Paper Products Ltd

ISBN 978 1 406217 94 0 (hardback)
14 13 12 11 10
10 9 8 7 6 5 4 3 2 1

ISBN 978 1 406218 02 2 (paperback)
14 13 12 11
10 9 8 7 6 5 4 3 2

British Library Cataloguing in Publication Data
A full catalogue record for this book is available from the British Library.

CONTENTS

CHAPTER 1

A FINAL TEST 4

CHAPTER 2

BAT-SIGNAL BEGINNINGS...........10

CHAPTER 3

LEARNING TO ADAPT 21

CHAPTER 4

NECESSARY DISTRACTIONS 28

CHAPTER 5

FINDING THE JEWEL THIEF 37

POLICE FILE 50
BIOGRAPHIES.....................52
GLOSSARY 53
DISCUSSION QUESTIONS...........54
WRITING PROMPTS...............55

A FINAL TEST

Tim Drake was excited. As he adjusted the mask on his face, he stood in the Batcave, feeling ready to take on the world.

For the last six months, he had been training his mind and body to become the next ally in Batman's fight against crime.

"When do we go on patrol?" the boy asked his mentor.

Batman did not answer. He was taking supplies from a metal cabinet and adding them to his Utility Belt.

From the back, the cloaked super hero seemed ominous, even scary, as he stood in the caverns beneath Wayne Manor.

"Well?" prodded Tim.

"You completed your training with the best teachers I could find," Batman said. His voice echoed off the rocky walls. "But that doesn't mean I think you're ready."

"What will convince you?" Tim asked.

"A final test," Batman replied.

"Okay," Tim said. "What do you have in mind?"

Finished with his task, the Dark Knight slowly turned around. The expression under his cowl was unreadable.

"Hide and seek," Batman said.

Tim's jaw dropped open in surprise.

"A kid's game?" Tim asked.

"Not quite," Batman said. "I will be hiding somewhere in Gotham City. There will be one clue at the starting point, and you will have until midnight to find me."

Tim started to protest, but Batman held up his hand. "After all, it's a school night," said the Dark Knight.

Tim shuffled his feet. This wasn't what he had expected after months of mastering martial arts, forensics, and science, all while still attending secondary school.

"Fine," he agreed. "When do we begin?"

"Right now," Batman said. "And your chaperone has just arrived."

Tim's eyes narrowed. "Why do I need a babysitter?" he asked. "Who is it? Alfred?"

Batman shook his head. A figure appeared from the shadows, dressed in blue and black, his outfit inspired by Batman's own suit. Tim was surprised to see Dick Grayson, the crime fighter known as Nightwing. He had been the first Robin.

"Hello, Tim," Nightwing said, his face breaking into a grin. "This should be fun."

"Maybe for you," Tim said.

CHAPTER 2

BAT-SIGNAL BEGINNINGS

While Batman drove the Batmobile into the city, Tim sat in the passenger seat. He was ready. He was confident. He knew he would always honour the uniform. Did he really need this final test? Well, if it meant only one more night before officially becoming Robin, then he thought he could get through it!

The sleek, dark vehicle parked in an alley near Police Headquarters. Batman leaped out of the car. "Wait five minutes," he said. "Then check the roof."

The Dark Knight soared away, his cape fluttering in the evening breeze.

As Tim watched Batman vanish from sight, he heard a sound and looked up. Nightwing was waiting for him on a fire escape. He had a big grin on his face.

"What's so funny?" Tim asked in an irritated voice.

"When he tested me," Nightwing said, "I was just as anxious as you are now."

"Really?" Tim asked.

Nightwing nodded. Then, he crouched and expertly launched himself across the alley to a narrow windowsill. Tim broke into a smile of his own. He leaped out of the Batmobile and grabbed the ladder of the fire escape. Quickly, he made his way up to where Nightwing was waiting for him.

"So," the older of the two began, "where did Batman hide the clue?"

Tim jerked a thumb over his shoulder at the next building. "Police Headquarters," explained Tim. "Batman said the clue would be on the roof."

Tim positioned himself on a railing of the fire escape. He threw his Batarang up towards the police building's flagpole.

CLINK The Batarang and its rope coiled around the base of the pole. Tim tugged the rope once to test its strength, and then launched himself into the air.

Tim enjoyed the warm breeze that rushed against his face as he swung over the alley and towards the roof.

As he landed on the rooftop, he heard Nightwing touch down beside him.

Sure enough, placed directly on top of the unlit Bat-Signal was the clue. It was a playing card – the ace of diamonds.

Tim walked over and examined it without touching the card. Nightwing followed, watching in silence.

Tim took a special light from his belt and shone it on the card. He clicked it off and looked over at Nightwing. "Looks new," he said. "No fingerprints or identifying marks, of course."

"A playing card could mean the Joker," Tim said, thinking aloud. "But I doubt we're going after him as part of the test. The card has to mean something else."

Tim's eyes scanned the rooftop. In the south-west corner, he spotted a single footprint in the dirt and dust.

"Which way, kid?" Nightwing asked.

"Towards the Hill," Tim said, referring to a particularly dangerous part of the city. "The footprint points in that direction."

"What about the playing card?" questioned Nightwing.

"I still need some time to think about that," Tim said. He threw his Batarang into the air. Nightwing followed suit.

Tim crouched on the edge of the roof, ready to swing away, but Nightwing grabbed his arm and pointed. Tim looked and saw a cluster of people standing at a nearby street corner.

"Got it," Tim said.

The pair of heroes swung towards the people, away from the direction of the Hill.

A moment later, they landed on the street and released their ropes.

Three men in leather jackets were robbing an elderly couple, who cowered in fear. Nightwing crept up behind them and tapped one thug on the shoulder. As the thief turned, a fist met his jaw. **WHAM!**

Tim tackled another mugger, knocking him to the ground. **THUD!** With calm, practised ease, he whipped out a pair of plastic handcuffs from his Utility Belt and secured the man's wrists. **CLICK!**

Suddenly, the last remaining thug charged at Nightwing with his fist raised.

Tim quickly sprang to his feet and pulled a Batarang out from his Utility Belt. Then he tossed the Batarang at the attacking thief's arm.

Nightwing quickly tackled the thief, subduing him. He looked up at Tim, and said, "Nice one, kid."

Tim beamed with pride.

"Thank you so much," the woman said in a weak voice. "You two are almost as good as Batman!" added her husband.

"Almost," said Nightwing, grinning.

Tim radioed the police and then turned to his partner. "It's getting late," he said. "We need to keep moving."

Nightwing nodded, and once more they were on their way to the Hill.

"Well, it wasn't exactly taking down Two-Face, but I'm glad we could help," Tim said.

"Crime is crime," said Nightwing.

Nightwing's smile suddenly froze as he looked into the distance. Tim followed his gaze and saw blinking lights from two cars that had smashed into one another. Nightwing shot Tim a glance.

"I know, I know," Tim grumbled. "We have to make another detour."

They rushed to the scene of the accident and surveyed the damage. One of the drivers had got out and seemed dazed. The other car was more seriously damaged and a woman was trapped in it.

Tim rushed to the side of the car. The metal door had been twisted and it could not be opened. The woman watched with wide eyes as Tim leaped on to the hood. Tim gestured for her to remain calm. He pulled out a device from his Utility Belt and aimed it at the windscreen. *BZZT!*

The device shot out a bright red laser beam. Swiftly, Tim cut around the windscreen and tossed it aside.

Once there was an opening, Tim eased into the car and used the laser to puncture the airbag. By then, Nightwing had moved to the bonnet. He helped his young ally pull the thankful woman to freedom.

Sirens in the distance told them help was on the way.

CHAPTER 3

LEARNING TO ADAPT

As the paramedics tended to the crash victims, Tim and Nightwing continued their way towards the Hill.

"It's already after ten," Tim complained.

"Would you rather have left that woman in the car?" Nightwing asked, as they ran along the rooftops above the city.

"Of course not," Tim replied.

Tim turned his mind back to the playing card that Batman had left. He wondered if a card factory was located in the Hill.

"Our job isn't just about arresting super-villains," Nightwing continued.

"I know, it's just – it's my first night, and I want it to count," Tim said. "I want to find Batman and earn his approval."

"When Batman tested me, I was just as excited as you are," Nightwing said. "But you have to be patient and learn to adapt when things don't go as planned."

Tim looked up at Nightwing and nodded. He knew Dick's advice was good. Nightwing knew more than most people about things going bad.

Tim remembered that Dick Grayson had once been a member of the famous Flying Graysons circus troupe. While performing in Gotham, his parents had fallen to their deaths.

Their trapeze ropes had been cut by criminals who were trying to scare the circus owner into giving them money.

Bruce Wayne had been at the circus that day. As Batman, he comforted the weeping eight-year-old. Having been an orphan of crime himself, Batman took the boy into his home and raised him as his own son.

Years later, Dick had begged Batman for a chance at finding the criminal boss who had caused his parents' deaths. Batman knew that Dick was strong and athletic, so he agreed.

Batman gave Dick a colourful uniform, naming him Robin. The duo eventually tracked down and arrested the criminal who was responsible. It was only afterwards that Dick had begun the rest of his training as a crime fighter.

Tim Drake had been lucky. His parents were still alive when they had taken him to see the Graysons perform on that fateful night. Later in life, he saw Robin performing a stunt that the acrobatic family had once done. It was then that Tim realized that Dick Grayson was Robin.

Dick grew up and became Nightwing, leaving Batman to fight crime on his own. Tim was convinced that Batman needed a new partner – a second Robin. He proved he was worthy by revealing the secrets he solved to Batman, who was impressed. Dick gave Tim his approval, which helped decide the matter.

To become the new Robin, Tim had to accept six long months of difficult training. He was schooled in gymnastics, martial arts, escapology, and forensics.

Tim's training had been intense, but the young crime fighter had been up to the task. Stealing time to secretly train with Batman had been easy, too, since Tim's parents were constantly travelling.

However, while Tim's parents had been away on business, a villain called the Obeah Man kidnapped the couple for ransom. Batman rushed to the Caribbean to save them, but he was too late. Tim's mother had died. He did manage to rescue his dad, Jack, who had been injured.

Now, Tim was caring for his father, who was undergoing physical therapy. Between helping his father and secretly training with Batman, Tim had almost no free time.

Fortunately, the Drake home was near Wayne Manor, so visiting the Batcave had been easy enough.

Tim had trained hard. He was ready. All he had to do now was find Batman within the next hour to become the new Robin.

CRASH!! A noise interrupted Tim's thoughts. He swivelled his head around, searching for the source. There, in a park's playground, a gang fight had begun.

"Nightwing!" he called.

"I see it," his partner said.

The two leaped to a nearby rooftop and observed the scene. Tim counted the number of fighters.

"There are a dozen of them," he said.

"Good, six for each of us!" Nightwing said, ready for some action.

Tim nodded, and the two heroes leaped into yet another necessary distraction.

CHAPTER 4

NECESSARY DISTRACTIONS

The gang members, one group wearing red bandanas and the other wearing green ones, were so busy fighting with each other that no one noticed the costumed heroes.

Nightwing grabbed one gang member by his leather jacket and pulled him away from the others. "Don't you know the noise is keeping the neighbours up?" he asked with a smirk.

The boy tried to land a punch, but Nightwing was faster. He caught the thug's fist in his open hand. WHAM!

"I think you've had enough fun for tonight," Nightwing added. He picked up the thug and tossed him into some bushes.

Tim laughed and then threw himself into the middle of the brawl. Crouching low, he spun in a circle by the gangsters. He used his left leg to sweep their feet, tripping several fighters to the ground.

He and Nightwing quickly separated the gangsters, removing their weapons one by one. Suddenly disarmed, the two groups just stood there, breathing heavily, staring at the masked duo.

"We could keep this up all night," Nightwing said. "But you guys can't. You're sloppy and undisciplined."

"This isn't your fight," said one of the boys. He wore a red bandana.

"True," Tim agreed. "But now it's no one's fight. This is about turf, right? The Red Fists want control of the park, which the Green Flames have claimed for years."

One gangster, and then another, nodded in agreement.

"Your leaders need to settle this dispute and keep the peace," Tim continued. "Or we will be back."

"That's it? You're leaving us?" one of the boys asked.

Tim walked closer, and the guy took a step backwards. "The police have already been called by neighbours watching from the flats," Tim said. "Start fighting again, and all of you will get arrested. Now get out of here and call it a night."

The boys drifted away, one by one.

"Good work," Nightwing said, placing a hand on Tim's shoulder.

"Thanks, but now it's after eleven o'clock," replied Tim. "We have to get a move on if I have any chance of finding Batman."

He turned to leave, but then paused when he heard a soft sound. Someone was crying, and it wasn't a gang member.

Carefully, he walked towards a cluster of trees in the corner of the park. As Tim neared them, he slowed down. He saw a whimpering young child.

"It's okay. I'm a friend," Tim said softly.

The young girl was hiding between a tree and a chain-link fence. She had been crying for quite some time. She was shivering in the cold night air.

"What's your name?" asked Tim.

"Elizabeth," she said between sobs.

"Are you lost?" Tim asked.

"Yes," Elizabeth said, sniffling.

"I can help you," Tim said. He extended one hand towards her. She considered it for a moment, staring at his black mask. Then she met his hand with her own.

The two walked away from the trees towards the better-lit central area of the park. Nightwing stood there, returning his radio to his side.

"I've already called the police to help find her parents," he said.

"Thanks," Tim said, squeezing the girl's hand. She had stopped crying and was now staring at Nightwing in awe.

"Are you Batman?" the girl asked Nightwing. "Where's your cape?"

Tim chuckled. "No, that's his friend Nightwing," Robin said. "Batman's missing, and we're looking for him."

"He's lost like me?" she asked.

"Not quite," Tim said. "He's hiding."

"You'd better find him," Elizabeth said. "Mum says we need him."

"Very true," Tim said.

It took a few minutes before the police arrived. It was nearly midnight. Tim hid his concern about the time from the girl.

Instead, Tim asked Elizabeth about where her parents lived, to make it easier for the police to take her home.

A uniformed officer arrived shortly after. Tim told the officer everything the little girl had told him about her home and her parents. The officer led Elizabeth away while Tim waved goodbye.

Once they had left, Tim turned to Nightwing. The older hero was listening to his radio with a frown on his face.

"Now what?" asked Tim.

"A jewellery shop alarm just sounded not too far away," said Nightwing. "It sounds like a break-in."

Tim sighed and said, "I know. I know. We have to go and help."

CHAPTER 5

FINDING THE JEWEL THIEF

The young heroes seemed to be in a friendly race to beat each other to the jewellery shop. Soon, Tim and Nightwing were standing side by side, looking down at the streets from a rooftop.

Tim didn't hear any sirens from the top of the building. He suspected the police were still busy dealing with the gangs and the lost girl.

"Looks like it's just us," Tim said.

"What do you see?" Nightwing asked.

"The jewel thieves must have entered through the rear door," Tim explained. "No lookouts. No getaway car. They must be hoping to grab the jewels and just walk away."

"Sounds about right," Nightwing agreed. "What do we do?"

"Wait for them to come out rather than wreck the shop," Tim said with confidence.

"Let's get in position," Nightwing said. He ran along the rooftop to reach a spot above the rear entrance of the jewellery shop. Tim followed, feeling better about the situation.

As the two watched and waited, a large shadow appeared in the doorway.

Without hesitation, Tim launched himself off the rooftop.

Tim swung down the building with practised ease. Halfway to the ground, he kicked hard off the concrete wall and flipped backwards, releasing the rope.

Tim landed a few metres from the thief. He stood in front of the masked man.

"You can drop the jewels and let me cuff you," Tim suggested. "Or you can fight – and lose."

The man was tall and broad. He was wearing a black trench coat and a balaclava. His gloved hand stuffed a bag into his coat's deep pocket.

When his hand came back out, it was holding a long, glimmering knife. He crouched and then lunged forward. His knife was pointed directly at Tim.

"Fight it is," Tim said, flexing his legs.

Tim flipped backwards. **THWACK!**
His feet kicked the knife out of the man's
hand. As Tim landed, the unarmed
criminal rushed at him again. The man
wrapped his bulky arms around Tim
in a bear hug. The man squeezed with
surprising strength. Tim couldn't breathe,
and his sides began to hurt.

THUD! Tim stomped his right boot
heel into the attacker's foot. The man's grip
loosened. Tim crouched, slipping from his
arms. Then Tim sprang up and rammed his
head into the thief's jaw. That sent the man
falling backwards. Tim stood with his arms
crossed, standing over the man.

He smiled and said, "Game's over, Bruce.
I've found you." With that, he reached out
and pulled off the balaclava, revealing the
face of Bruce Wayne.

"When did you work it out?" Bruce asked.

"Well, let's start with your general build. You made no attempt to hide that," Tim said. "Then there was the fact that you were doing this entirely on foot, late at night without a crowd to hide in. Then, when I attacked you, two things happened. Nightwing stayed back, even though earlier tonight he helped me fight some criminals. Then there was the fact that you didn't even try to punch me – you didn't want to hurt your star pupil."

"Anything else?" Bruce asked.

Tim thought for a moment. "Yeah," he said. "You pulled out a knife when most thieves would have used a gun. Batman never uses a gun, even when playing hide and seek."

"And?" asked Batman, staring at him.

Tim blinked uncertainly.

Nightwing cleared his throat to attract Tim's attention. He pointed to the name on the sign above them: Ace Jewellery Shop.

Tim's eyes widened under his mask.

"Of course!" Tim exclaimed. "The ace of diamonds – the first clue."

By now, Batman was back on his feet. He was relocking the door to the shop.

"You pointed me in this direction," Tim continued, "but I kept getting distracted."

Batman gave him a puzzled look, so Tim recounted all the times he and Nightwing had to take detours.

Nightwing added, "Tim never rushed in foolishly. He was always patient."

Nightwing continued, "He studied the situation and determined what needed to be done. He looked for clues. He tried to resolve a fight through words, not fists. Pretty good work for his first night."

When Nightwing had finished, Batman nodded and cracked a rare smile.

"Then tonight you learned the most valuable lesson," Bruce said.

Tim nodded slowly. "We have to protect everyone," Tim said.

"Right," said Batman. "The police are good at what they do, but even they have their limits. Whenever possible, we support their efforts to keep Gotham safe."

Nightwing walked over to Tim and ruffled his hair. "I was a lot like you when I first started," he said.

"I thought every night would be spent chasing Catwoman and the Joker – nothing else. But sometimes it's more rewarding to help a lost child."

"You've learned a lot tonight," Batman said. He opened his trench coat to reveal his Batsuit underneath. Placing the cowl over his face, Bruce Wayne was once more the Dark Knight. "You showed compassion, you were calm under pressure, and you studied the facts before acting. You've learned your lessons well."

"Now?" Tim asked eagerly.

"Now you can go on active duty . . . Robin," Batman said to his new partner.

"Yes!" Tim exclaimed.

"My work here is done," Nightwing said. "You'll make a great replacement, Robin."

Nightwing and Batman shook hands. Then Nightwing jumped, grabbed a window ledge, climbed to the rooftops, and vanished from sight.

Moments later, two arms shot their grapnel guns into the sky. A pair of dark figures took flight above the streets, ready to protect Gotham City together.

Nightwing

REAL NAME: Dick Grayson

OCCUPATION: Policeman, crime fighter

BASE: Bludhaven

HEIGHT:
1 m 77 cm

WEIGHT:
79 kg

EYES:
Blue

HAIR:
Black

Dick Grayson was a member of the Flying Graysons, a family of circus acrobats. After Dick's parents were murdered, Bruce Wayne adopted the troubled youth. Grayson was determined to catch the criminals who had killed his parents, and he asked Batman to train him to become a super hero. Dick showed a lot of talent in his training, impressing the Dark Knight. Soon, Batman made Grayson the first Robin, and the two paired up to fight crime. Later, Dick made his own super hero costume by adding touches to Batman's suit. Nightwing was born.

Robin

REAL NAME: Tim Drake

OCCUPATION: Pupil, crime fighter

BASE: Gotham City

HEIGHT:
1 m 55 cm

WEIGHT:
52 kg

EYES:
Blue

HAIR:
Black

Tim got his chance to become the next Robin when Dick Grayson, the previous Robin, became Nightwing. Tim, quite brilliant for his age, discovered the secret identities of Nightwing *and* Batman. He approached Grayson and shared his discovery, impressing him. With Dick's approval, Batman accepted Tim into the Bat family and gave him the Robin mantle. As the current Robin, Tim Drake soars alongside Batman as one half of the Dynamic Duo, fighting against the criminal elements of Gotham City.

BIOGRAPHIES

Robert Greenberger began his career at Starlog Press. He then joined DC Comics as an assistant editor and eventually became Manager of Editorial Operations. In 2001, he became Marvel's Director of Publishing Operations. In 2002, he went back to DC Comics as a Senior Editor in its collected editions department. Bob then joined *Weekly World News* as Managing Editor until 2007. Since then, he has been a full-time freelance writer and editor. Bob has written many short works of fiction, including *The Essential Batman Encyclopedia* and *Batman Vault*. Bob lives with his wife, Deb, and their dog, Dixie.

Since he was 11 years old, **Gregg Schigiel** has wanted to be a cartoonist. Gregg has worked on projects featuring Batman, Spider-Man, SpongeBob SquarePants, and just about everything in between.

Lee Loughridge has been working in comics for more than 14 years. He currently lives in a tent on the beach.

GLOSSARY

acrobatic difficult gymnastic movement usually done in the air

adapt change because of a new situation or experience

adjust move or change something slightly

balaclava woollen hat that covers the head and neck

compassion feeling of sympathy for someone

cower crouch in fear or shame

cowl large, loose hood

deduce work something out from clues or from what you already know

escapology art of breaking free from ropes, handcuffs, and chains

grapnel hook with iron claws attached to a rope

ominous feeling that something bad is going to happen

subduing defeating someone in battle, or calming and controlling something

DISCUSSION QUESTIONS

1. Which is more important – protecting the innocent, or catching criminals? Why?

2. Nightwing, Robin, and Batman each have their own costumes and personalities. If you could be a super hero, which one would you want to be like?

3. Robin and Nightwing help a lost child. Have you ever helped someone?

WRITING PROMPTS

1. More than anything, Robin wants to be respected and treated like an adult. Have you ever felt like you were being treated like a child? How did it make you feel? Write about it.

2. Write another chapter to this book where Robin fights crime on his own. What kinds of criminals does he catch? What super-villain does he fight? You decide.

3. Robin has to go through intense training to become a super hero. Have you ever had to do something difficult? Write about your experience.

MORE NEW
BATMAN
ADVENTURES!

KILLER CROC HUNTER

**TWO-FACE'S
DOUBLE TAKE**

**BAT-MITE'S
BIG BLUNDER**

**CATWOMAN'S
CLASSROOM OF CLAWS**

ARCTIC ATTACK